Little Bat

WRITTEN BY TANIA COX

ILLUSTRATED BY ANDREW MCLEAN

SCHOLASTIC INC.
New York Toronto London Auckland Sydney
Mexico City New Delhi Hong Kong

Little Bat was nervous.

She'd never done this before.

"You'll be fine, Little Bat," said Mom.

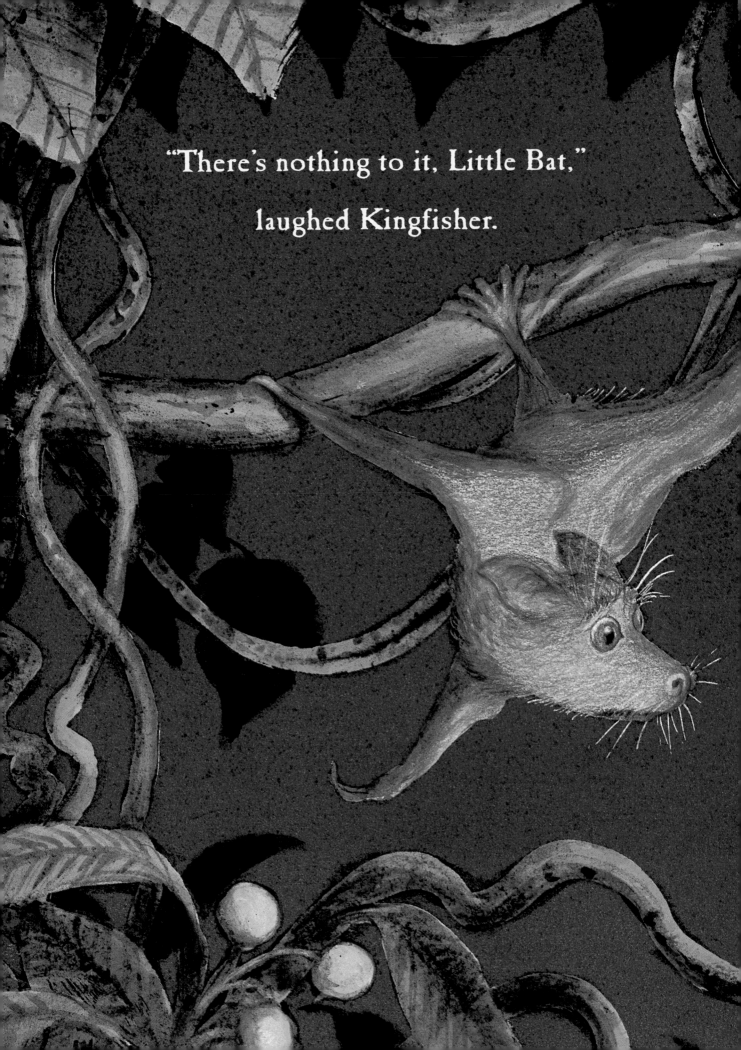

"There's nothing to it, Little Bat,"
laughed Kingfisher.

"Just take a deep breath, Little Bat,"

hissed Dragon.

"And do what comes naturally, Little Bat,"

urged Possum.

"Don't go too fast, Little Bat,"

squawked Parrot.

"Or too far, Little Bat," hooted Owl.

"And keep your eyes open, Little Bat,"

warned Butterfly.

"Have fun, Little Bat!" sang Sunbird.

"Good luck, Little Bat," cheered Quoll.

"I wish I could come too, Little Bat,"

sighed Python.

"Go on, Little Bat," whispered Mom.

"You can do it. You really can."

"I can do it," squeaked Little Bat. "I really can . . ."

. . . flyyyy!"

ISBN 0-439-26210-0

Text copyright © 2000 by Tania Cox.
Illustrations copyright © 2000 by Andrew McLean. All rights reserved.
Published by Scholastic Inc., 555 Broadway, New York, NY 10012,
by arrangement with Working Title Press. SCHOLASTIC and
associated logos are trademarks and/or registered trademarks
of Scholastic Inc.

12 11 10 9 8 7 6 5 4 3 2 1   1 2 3 4 5 6/0

Printed in the U.S.A.   14

First Scholastic printing, September 2001

Designed and typeset in Caslon Antique by Liz Nicholson, design BITE, Adelaide.

DEDICATION

With love and thanks to Ann James and Ann Haddon — T.C.

To Shaun and Scott — A.McL.

Andrew McLean used wax crayon and coloured ink, pencil and
pastel for the illustrations in this book.

The animals featured in this story are found in various parts of
Australia's north-eastern rainforests. They include the Little Red
Flying-fox, Buff-breasted Paradise-Kingfisher, Boyd's Forest
Dragon, Green Ringtail Possum, King Parrot, Lesser Sooty Owl,
Ulysses Butterfly, Yellow-breasted Sunbird, Spotted-tailed Quoll
and Green Python.